Chippee the Chicken

Longing for a Different Life

Jill A. Hawes

Illustrations by Trudy G. Hughes

Literacy & Life Consulting, LLC

This book is dedicated to Ms. Heather Curry and
Her Second Grade Class at Mt. Bethel Elementary, Cobb County Schools

and to

Jessica Appleyard, Principal of Mt. Bethel Elementary

Chippee the Chicken:
Longing for a Different Life

Copyright © 2020 by Jill A. Hawes
Illustrations by Trudy G. Hughes

Published by:
Literacy & Life Consulting, LLC

ISBN 978-1-7350296-0-3 Paperback
ISBN 978-1-7350296-1-0 eBook

Library of Congress Control Number: 2020908735

Printed in the United States of America

Chippee was born a chicken. She was born in a box with an artificial light and an artificial heater. Chippee hatched next to other chickens who chirped happily and loved being in the warm, cozy, safe box.

"Cock-a-doodle-do, this is a great life!" exclaimed her big brother chicken. "We are well fed and receive fresh water every day!"

"And it is so warm and cozy in here!" added one of her sister chickens.

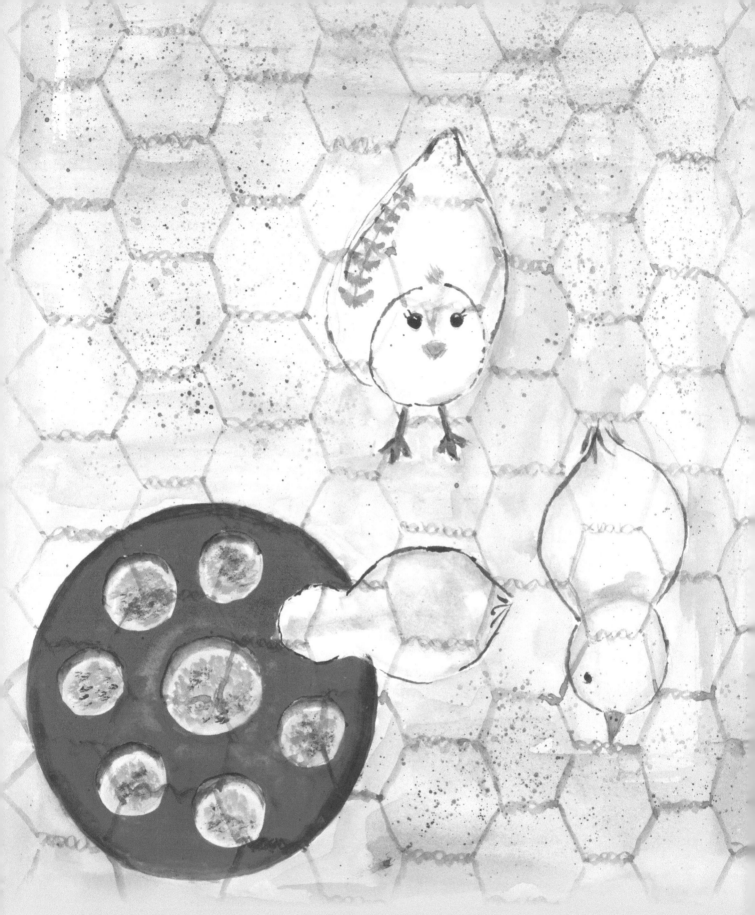

"Humph," Chippee thought, "I don't think this is such a great life! We are trapped in this box with nothing to do except eat, drink, and chirp. I long for a different life!"

And on that day, Chippee made a decision in her heart. "I am not going to settle for this hum-drum life with this family of chickens. I long for a different life!"

So...Chippee hatched a plan.

A plan of escape.

A PLAN of FREEDOM!

Every day the teacher lifted the box top to put in food and fresh water. Chippee heard the teacher say, "Children, come and see how the chicks are growing! Be very careful that you don't disturb them."

The children gathered around, peered into the box, and talked softly to Chippee and her brothers and sisters. They said things like, "Ahh, look at the chicks. They are so cute! May we touch them?"

Sometimes the teacher lifted a few of the chicks out of the box to play with the children. The other chicks nervously chirped out warnings to each other, "Be careful, they will be too rough and will hurt us!"

But Chippee was not nervous at all. She looked at her brother and sister chickens and ruffled her feathers at them, "Life is an adventure, and YOU are missing it!"

Chippee LOVED being out of the box and playing with the students on the floor! She often scampered into their laps and took a nap. "Ahhhh, this is where I belong," sighed Chippee.

Always too soon, the teacher picked Chippee up and put her back in the warm box with the lid securely fastened.

As time went on, Chippee became more and more uncomfortable in the box with her brother and sister chickens. They chirped and played together. Her older brother chicken would try to include her. "Chippee, come join us as we learn to scratch for seed together and dream of our lives as chickens."

Chippee refused to join in, "No, thank you. I have better things to do!"

So…Chippee hatched a plan. A plan of escape. A PLAN of FREEDOM!

Chippee spent her time exercising her wings, building her flapping muscles, and increasing her flight endurance strength. Waiting…waiting… waiting for the opportune time to gain her freedom.

One day, the perfect time came at last! The students lined up at the door to go to art class. The children were quiet as they filed into the hall.

But Chippee wasn't quiet! She knew this was the time to join the children and escape! She flew up, up, up and hit the screen top on the box where she lived with her brothers and sisters. "There they gooooo!" Chippee cried out. She was desperate! She flew up, up, up and banged against the bottom of the screen.

Breathless, she tried again and again. Suddenly, the box lid moved. A whoosh of air came pouring in…the corner of the screen was open. Quickly Chippee flew to the corner…up, up, up… and then WHOA…down, down, down…. Kerplunk! She landed on the floor!

She ran, flew, ran…huffing and puffing, chirping down the hall after the children, "Wait for me!"

She was...FREEEEEE!

But…then…the teacher heard her chirps of excitement. The teacher smiled, gently lifted her up, kissed her head, and put her back in the box with her brothers and sisters.

Chippee's brothers and sisters scolded her, laughed at her attempt to escape, and pecked at her.

"Stop causing trouble, stay where you belong!" insisted one of her sister chickens.

"What are you searching for?" asked another sister.

"YOU are a CHICKEN," crowed her older brother loudly. "ACT like a CHICKEN!"

Chippee was not only humiliated, she was sore from all the pecking. She cowered in the box. "I was free, but here I am imprisoned in the very life I want to escape!"

So…Chippee hatched a plan. A plan of escape.
A PLAN of FREEDOM!

Time went on…and the teacher allowed Chippee more time out of the box. The teacher often let her sit at the reading table while the children read their books. Chippee was content sitting and listening to the stories they read aloud and often she would nod off to sleep.

This was the life! She was away from her brothers and sisters, and the children loved having her with them.

Then one day, life changed again. The teacher placed Chippee and her brothers and sisters in a bigger box and put them in her car. The teacher lifted Chippee out of the box and let the children see her one last time. Chippee chirped her good-byes to the children. The children had tears in their eyes as they waved and cried, "Good-bye, Chippee. We will miss you soooo much!"

The trip seemed long; however, Chippee didn't mind. The teacher let Chippee sit on her lap as she drove. Chippee enjoyed the fresh air streaming through the window and the sunlight warming her feathers.

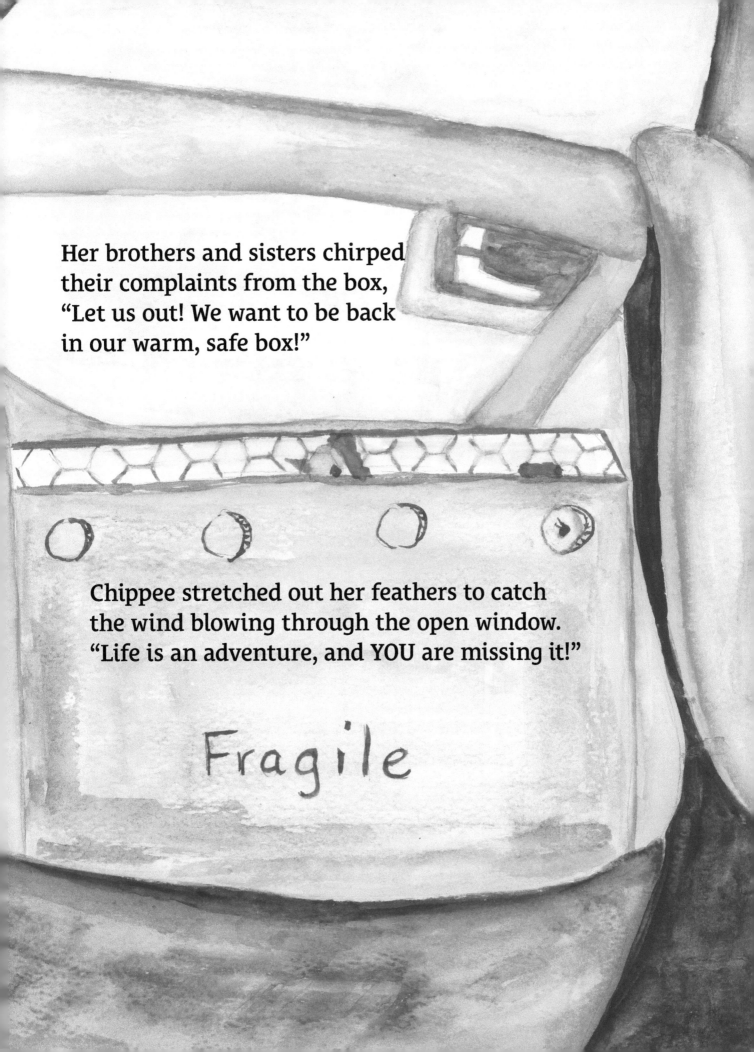

Her brothers and sisters chirped
their complaints from the box,
"Let us out! We want to be back
in our warm, safe box!"

Chippee stretched out her feathers to catch
the wind blowing through the open window.
"Life is an adventure, and YOU are missing it!"

Fragile

The teacher turned onto a dirt-covered road. Chippee saw a big house with lots of strange creatures running around outside. The teacher announced, "This is your new home! It's called a farm and is full of all kinds of animals. You are going to love it here!"

A smiling man in a straw hat approached the car. The teacher announced, "Here comes the farmer. He will take good care of all of you."

The teacher placed the box of chickens at the farmer's feet. She tried to hand Chippee to him. Chippee flapped and fluttered to stay in the teacher's arms.

The teacher then explained the chicken situation.

"This is Chippee. She is a very special chicken. She doesn't like being with her chicken family. They fly at her and peck at her and don't include her in their chicken family. So Chippee spent a lot of time with the children instead. She LOVES being with the children and doesn't consider herself a chicken at all."

The farmer frowned and told the teacher that Chippee had made a mistake. "She spent so much time with the children that Chippee didn't think of herself as a chicken any longer, which could lead to a dangerous life."

The teacher was shocked! "Oh no," she gasped, "what will happen to Chippee now?"

The farmer reassured her, "I will take special care of Chippee. I will build her a special coop where she can live alone for a while in a safe place away from her brothers and sisters."

He went on, "Then I will gradually reintroduce her to her brothers and sisters. I will teach her how to get along with her chicken family as a chicken."

The teacher was so relieved. She kissed Chippee on the head and whispered her final good-bye. As her car pulled off, she rolled down the window and waved at Chippee's brothers and sisters. A tear dripped off Chippee's beak as she watched the dust flying off the tires of the teacher's departing car.

"Back in a box," Chippee wept. "This one is bigger and outside, but I'm still trapped in a box!"

Chippee watched her brothers and sisters running in the yard and going into their house together. They were content to live the warm, safe life. Chippee longed for a different life.

So…Chippee hatched a plan. A plan of escape. A PLAN of FREEDOM!

Chippee took her eyes off her brothers and sisters and began watching the farmer instead. She watched him go through his daily chores of feeding all the animals. "What a boring life," Chippee thought.

Then the farmer did something unusual. He went into the house and came out carrying a large suitcase. He climbed into his red pickup truck and sped down the dirt road away from the farm.

Chippee waited until the afternoon to see
if the farmer would return. He didn't.

So...Chippee hatched a plan. A plan of escape.
A PLAN of FREEDOM!

A few days later, the animals heard the rumble of the farmer's truck speeding down the dirt road. The farmer got out of his truck and greeted all the animals. He then ventured toward Chippee's coop to see how she was doing.

"Chippee, come out of your chicken house," called the farmer.

"Chippee, oh Chippee, here chick, chick, chick," sang the farmer.

But there was no Chippee in sight.

The farmer scratched his head in wonderment as he lifted the gate latch. He bent down and peered into the chicken coop. "Chippee?" said the farmer.

Still no Chippee in sight.

Suddenly, the farmer's eyes dropped to the bottom of the coop. What he saw astonished him....

There was one feather lying on the bottom of the coop among the chicken seeds.

Chippee was gone!

Bewildered, the farmer walked slowly out of the coop shaking his head. He whispered to himself, "What could have happened to Chippee? Where did she go?"

He walked into the farmhouse and decided to call the teacher.

The cell phone jiggled in the teacher's pocket as she finished her last reading group. She took it out and immediately recognized the phone number. She said quietly under her breath, "I wondered when the farmer might call."

As the farmer gently broke the news to the teacher about Chippee's disappearance, the teacher just smiled.

Sitting quietly in the corner of the classroom with the other children was Chippee, reading a book herself and enjoying the freedom of being with the family she had grown to love.